Enid Blyton

You're a Nuisance Mister Meddle

Text illustrations by Stephen Dell
Cover illustration by Maggie Downer

D1340597

AWARD PUBLICATIONS LIMITED

Enid Blyton's Happy Days!

Snowball the Pony

Bimbo and Topsy

Run-About's Holiday

The Adventures of Binkle and Flip

Binkle and Flip Misbehave

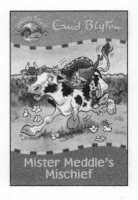

Mister Meddle's Mischief

Mister Meddle's Muddles

Merry Mister Meddle

You're a Nuisance Mister Meddle

Collect all the titles in the series!

The Adventures of
Mr Pink-Whistle

Mr Pink-Whistle
Has Some Fun

Mr Pink-Whistle's
Party

Mr Pink-Whistle
Interferes

Hello
Mr Twiddle!

Mr Twiddle
in Trouble Again

Don't Be Silly,
Mr Twiddle!

Mr Twiddle
in Trouble Again

Shuffle
the Shoemaker

For further information on Enid Blyton please visit *www.blyton.com*

ISBN 978-1-84135-653-2

First published 1950 & 1954 by George Newnes

First published by Award Publications Limited 2004
This edition first published 2010

Published by Award Publications Limited,
The Old Riding School, The Welbeck Estate,
Worksop, Nottinghamshire, S80 3LR

11 2

Printed in the United Kingdom

Contents

Chapter 1

You're a Nuisance Mr Meddle

One day Mr Meddle took a little walk round the village. It was a lovely sunny day, and he had on his new suit and felt rather proud of himself.

'I hope everyone notices my new suit,' he thought. 'Ah, good morning, Mrs Thump – what a lovely day! Oh, hello, Mrs Woolly, I hope I see you well! Ah, and here is dear Miss Scurry – how are you today?'

Nobody bothered to stop and talk to Meddle or to admire his new suit. He was very disappointed. He walked on and came to Mrs Puff's dear little cottage. Roses grew all over it, and in her garden were fruit trees of many

7

kinds. Ah – plums! Meddle saw them hanging purple and juicy on the trees.

He saw Mrs Puff at the front door, doing something to her roses. He decided to go and be polite to her – then she might offer him a basket of plums!

So in at the front gate he went. He took off his fine new hat and bowed. 'Good morning, Mrs Puff. What a lovely day!'

'Oh – it's you, Meddle,' said Mrs Puff, not sounding very pleased. 'How's your Aunt Jemima? She told me what a trial you are at times, meddling and muddling.'

'That wasn't very nice of her,' said Meddle,

offended. 'But she is often very difficult to please. Very!'

Mrs Puff stood on her tiptoes to try and reach a rose-spray that had got loose. 'There now!' she said. 'I knew I wouldn't be able to reach it.'

'Pray let me,' said Meddle, at once. 'In fact if I can do anything for you, dear Mrs Puff, I will – anything! I am always willing to help my aunt's friends.'

'I don't think I want your help, thank you, Meddle,' said Mrs Puff, hastily. She knew too well what a nuisance Mr Meddle could be when he tried to help. 'I'll get my husband to fetch the ladder and tie up that spray for me when he comes in. He's busy just now.'

She went into the house and shut the front door. 'Bother!' thought Meddle. 'She didn't offer me any plums – and I don't quite like to knock on the door and ask her for some. Well – I must be on my way, I suppose. What a pity she didn't notice my new suit!'

He was just walking down the path to the gate when he caught sight of a ladder in the garden. It was leaning against a plum tree, Mr Meddle stopped and looked at it.

Suppose he fetched it, put it against the

front porch, and neatly tied up that rose-spray for Mrs Puff – and a few others he could see were loose. Wouldn't she tell him to go and pick himself some nice plums for being so kind? Yes – surely she would!

Meddle went to fetch the ladder. It wasn't very heavy, so he put it over his shoulder and took it to the porch. He set it up and climbed it. He took some string from his pocket and began to tie up the rose spray, humming a little tune, and hoping that Mrs Puff would hear it.

He tied up quite a lot of sprays, but Mrs Puff didn't come out. Meddle was getting tired of standing on the ladder, tying up every spray within reach. He was tired of the roses, too – they had far too many thorns, and already he had torn his new suit in three places.

Then a loud voice shouted from somewhere. 'Hey! I want to get down! HEY!'

Meddle was surprised. Who wanted to get down? And why? He couldn't see anyone about.

The voice yelled again. 'I'm coming down! I've got enough now. HEY, I say – I want to get down!'

'Get down, then, whoever you are, and wherever you are!' shouted Meddle. 'Nobody's stopping you, are they?'

The front door opened and Mrs Puff appeared. 'Meddle! Are you still here? Whatever are you doing to my roses – good gracious, you've tied the sprays so tightly that they look simply dreadful. And where did you get that ladder?'

The loud voice yelled again from somewhere. 'HEY! Is that you, dear? I tell you, I want to get down. Did you take the ladder away? Well, bring it back!'

'Good gracious – that's Mr Puff, up the big

11

plum-tree,' said Mrs Puff. 'Meddle – did you take his ladder away? How *dare* you?'

'Er – well – I didn't know he was up the plum-tree,' said Meddle. 'I just took the ladder for the roses.'

'BRING BACK MY LADDER!' shouted Mr Puff, and Meddle got down the ladder in such a hurry that he caught his foot in one of the rungs and fell to the ground – bump! He got up and dusted himself.

'Take the ladder to Mr Puff,' said Mrs Puff, crossly. 'Really, Meddle, why must you always meddle in things that don't concern you! Now I'll have to untie all those sprays!'

Meddle ran to the big plum-tree with the ladder. He set it up against the tree. 'Sorry, Mr Puff!' he called. 'I just –'

'Oh – so it was you!' cried Mr Puff, and an angry red face appeared through the leaves. 'I might have guessed!' And, dear me, he threw a handful of ripe plums at poor Meddle! They burst all over his beautiful new suit.

Meddle fled. Mr Puff looked so very angry that he was quite sure he would get a whole lot more plums in half a second. He ran down the road and turned the corner. He almost bumped into his Aunt Jemima.

'Now, now – look where you are going!' she said. 'My goodness me, Meddle! Look at your clothes! Torn – and dusty – and stained with purple juice. How can you walk about like that? Why don't you go and buy yourself a really nice new suit? I'm ashamed of you!'

And away she walked, with her nose in the air. Poor Meddle – in trouble again! If only he didn't meddle in other people's business he'd be a lot better off, wouldn't he?

Chapter 2

Mr Meddle in a Fix

Mr Meddle arrived at his Aunt Jemima's hoping she would let him stay for a day or two. He had spent all his money, and he thought it would be such a good idea if he could live with his aunt for a little while.

'Good gracious – so you've turned up again!' said Aunt Jemima, in disgust, as Meddle came walking in at the door. 'Talk about a bad penny!'

'I don't know what you mean, Aunt,' said Meddle, surprised. 'I've come to see if I can be any help to you.'

'You can stay and have lunch with me if you go and fetch some parcels and packages I've left at the shops,' said Aunt Jemima. 'But you will leave immediately after dinner, Meddle – no staying on for weeks as you did last time.'

'Are there many parcels?' asked Meddle. He didn't like carrying a heavy load.

'Plenty,' said Aunt Jemima. 'There's a chair that's been mended – and a bag of carrots – and the kitchen clock – and a whole pile of smaller ones, too. I went to fetch them yesterday, but my little car broke down and I had to leave it at the garage to be seen to.'

'Is it mended yet?' asked Meddle, hopefully.

'It may be,' said his aunt. 'You can call in and see if you like – and run it home for me – but don't knock too many lamp-posts down on the way. They are expensive things to pay for. Unless, of course, you are feeling rather rich, Meddle, and don't mind.'

'I'm not feeling rich at all,' said Meddle, thinking of his empty pockets. 'Not in the least, I'll fetch your little car and all your parcels, Aunt, and I'll be back again in a jiffy.'

'I know your jiffies!' said his aunt. 'More like five or six hours! Well – I shan't wait for lunch, so just hurry up. Here is the list of shops I've left my parcels at. And if they want

you to pay for them, give them the money
and I'll pay you when you come back.'

Meddle walked off. 'Pay for her parcels! I
should think not!' he said to himself. 'For
one thing I can't, and for another thing if I
did do such a silly thing, Aunt Jemima
wouldn't pay me back – she'd say I owed her
money, anyway, which I suppose I do.

He went to the garage first. Ah, his aunt's
car was ready. Good. Meddle rather fancied
himself driving a car, and he got into the
driving-seat at once. Off he went at top speed,
nearly taking a petrol pump with him.

He came to the chair-mender's and
collected the chair, all neatly wrapped up in

sacking. The man didn't ask for payment so that was lucky. Meddle put the chair in the back of the car. Then he drove to the greengrocer's and got the bag of carrots.

'Fifty pence, please,' said the man, when he had put the carrots in at the back.

'Certainly,' said Meddle. 'Send the bill in to my aunt,' and he drove off before the man could take the carrots back again.

He got the kitchen clock, too, done up nicely in a cardboard box, marked 'This Way Up.' Not that Meddle took any notice of that at all. The clock had to stand on its head on the back seat.

It didn't like it at all, and began to strike very loudly indeed.

'All right, all right – don't keep telling me you are mended!' said Meddle. 'Be quiet!'

The smaller parcels had been left at the grocer's. There were a great many. 'I'll just take them out to my car now,' said Meddle, grandly.

'Certainly. That will be one pound, and thirty-four pence, please,' said the shop-woman, politely.

'Send in the bill,' said Meddle, picking up the parcels.

'Your Aunt Jemima always pays when she takes the things,' said the shop-woman firmly. 'I'd like the money, please.'

'Aunt Jemima will send it,' said Meddle, just as firmly, taking a step towards the door.

'Put those parcels down,' said the woman, suddenly angry. 'No money, no parcels!'

Meddle felt annoyed. Was he going to lose his nice lunch at his aunt's because of this exasperating woman? He really didn't know what to do.

Then the telephone bell rang and the woman hurried to the back of the shop to answer it. 'I'll be back in a moment,' she called to Meddle.

'Ah!' thought Meddle, 'now's my chance! I'll slip these things straight out to the car and be off before she has finished telephoning!'

He rushed out of the shop with the parcels swinging all round him. He ran to one of the cars outside, wrenched open the door and flung the parcels on to the back seat, hoping there would be room for them.

He slammed the door, and started up the engine. There was no sign of the shop-woman. Good – he would race off home straight away.

Off he went. He turned the corner, and sat back in glee. Good – he had all the parcels safely; he hadn't had to pay for any, and he had got Aunt Jemima's car back for her. She ought to be so pleased with him that she would let him stay at least a day or two, not just for lunch only.

'Toot-toot, parp-parp!' said a car loudly, behind him. Meddle looked back. He caught sight of an extremely angry face – a very fierce face indeed.

'What's the matter with him?' thought Meddle, alarmed. 'What's he hooting at me for? I haven't broken any road rules.'

'Toot-toot, parp-parp!' went the car, trying to catch up Meddle.

Meddle decided to go faster. He didn't like the look of that man in the car at all. He might be a robber of some sort. This was a very lonely road he was on – suppose the man got in front of him, and forced him into the hedge! He would be able to rob Meddle of all the parcels he had so carefully fetched!

So he went faster than ever, and the hedge spun past so quickly that it seemed just a green line and nothing more. The car rocked about dangerously – and still from behind came that angry, insistent hooting!

Meddle was sure that the man at the wheel was shaking his fist at him.

'Either a robber or quite mad,' thought Meddle, bouncing so hard in a rut that he almost fell off his seat. 'Well, well – I must say that my aunt's car is a very good one – much faster than I expected. Thank goodness it is faster than that robber's behind.'

Meddle shook off the man at last, tore down a side-street and came to a stop outside his aunt's house. No sign of that man, thank goodness. He pulled out all the parcels and staggered into the house with them. 'I'm back, Aunt,' he said. 'And here are all your parcels. Haven't I been quick? I got your car, too.'

'Well, that's splendid,' said his aunt, pleased. 'Undo the chair, will you? We need another. And put the kitchen clock on the mantelpiece. And you might get a few carrots out of the sack and I'll cook them for our lunch.'

Meddle began undoing the big parcels. Where was the mended chair? Funny – he couldn't seem to see it.

Meddle undid a large parcel and to his astonishment out came a wash-tub. He hadn't remembered collecting a wash-tub.

'Where did that come from?' said his aunt, in surprise. 'I never bought a wash-tub. And where is that mended chair? And do get the clock out, Meddle, I want to know the time.'

'You'll soon know it,' said Meddle, unpacking at top speed. 'It stood on the back seat and struck without stopping when I put it there.'

He unpacked a parrot-cage and a lamp-shade, an electric iron and a dog-basket. Aunt Jemima stared at everything in amazement.

'Where did you get these? Where's my chair and clock and carrots?' she asked.

'I can't imagine,' said Meddle, in a panic. 'The carrots were in a bag, and the clock struck, so I know it was there, and the legs of the chair stuck out, so I'm sure I fetched that. Oh, Aunt – there's been some very strange magic at work here!'

'Is there anything left in the car?' asked his aunt. Meddle was just going to say 'no' when there came a knock at the door.

Meddle went to answer it. Mr Plod the policeman stood there!

'Little question of that car outside,' said Mr Plod. 'It's been reported to me as stolen. Do you know how it got there?'

Meddle stared at the car he had left outside. 'That's Aunt Jemima's car,' he said. 'Don't be silly, policeman.'

'Ho! We'll soon see who's silly,' said Mr Plod. 'See that car's number? Well, it's the same as the one that belongs to Mr Grim, and it was stolen this morning. See?'

Meddle didn't see. He called loudly to his

aunt. 'Aunt Jemima! Do come, please, and tell the policeman this is your car. He says it's been stolen.'

Aunt Jemima came rushing out. She stared at the car, and then she stared at Meddle. 'Where's my car?' she cried. 'What have you done with it? That's not my car!'

'Just what I said, madam,' said Mr Plod. 'This is one that's been stolen. And what's more, madam, there were a whole lot of valuable things in it, too – an electric iron, a dog-basket, a wash-tub, a —'

'Parrot-cage, a lampshade,' went on Aunt Jemima, glaring at poor Meddle. 'Explain this, Meddle – and tell me exactly where my things are – especially the kitchen clock.'

Well, Meddle couldn't explain. He couldn't for the life of him think what had happened. Surely it was a bad dream!

'When this fellow came running out of the grocer's with a lot of parcels, what did he do but jump into Mr Grim's empty car standing by the kerb with a whole lot of others,' said Mr Plod, 'and away he went at sixty miles an hour! And Mr Grim jumped into his brother's car and chased him – but he got away.'

'Meddle!' said his aunt, amazed and shocked. 'Is this the way you behave nowadays?'

'No,' said Meddle, desperately. 'I suppose I – er – well, I just got into the wrong car, Aunt Jemima.'

'Officer,' said Aunt Jemima, turning to the solemn policeman, 'Give my apologies to Mr Grim. Ask him to come here and collect his car and his belongings – and beg him please to stay and have lunch with me so that my nephew can explain his extraordinary behaviour.'

'Very good, Madam,' said Mr Plod, with a grin, and away he went.

'Go and wash your hands for lunch,' said Aunt Jemima to Meddle. I've no doubt Mr Grim will soon be along.'

Meddle went into the kitchen. A delicious smell of stew came from there – and on the stove he could see some kind of pudding bubbling away.

Meddle didn't wash his hands. He tiptoed through the kitchen, and through the scullery, out of the back door, and down the garden, and then he jumped over the wall at the bottom.

It was a terrible pity, but he really felt he couldn't stay for lunch if Mr Grim was coming. He went down the lane, hoping he wouldn't meet anyone.

He doesn't know who's coming round the corner, on his way to have lunch with Aunt Jemima, pleased to have been invited. It's Mr Grim hurrying, hurrying – longing for a nice meal – longing for a nasty talk with Meddle. Look out, Meddle – you're just about to bump into Mr Grim – there – I knew you would!

Chapter 3

Mr Meddle Tries to Be Helpful

Meddle was staying with his Aunt Jemima and she was not very pleased with him. This was not surprising, for Meddle had filled the salt-cellars with sugar, quite by mistake, and had filled the sugar basin with salt. So they had both had porridge and salt, and egg and sugar, for breakfast.

'If only you'd be a bit more helpful instead of doing such silly things,' grumbled Aunt Jemima. 'My hand just longs to pinch you, Meddle, and a very little more silliness from you and I shan't be able to stop my hand from doing what it wants to.'

Meddle went as far from his aunt as he

could. Her hand was big and hard and strong. 'I'm very sorry, Aunt,' he said. 'But the sugar and salt did look so much alike, you see.'

'You didn't think of reading what was on the salt-tin, I suppose?' said Aunt Jemima. 'No – don't try to alter the salt and the sugar now – you'll only end in mixing them up together.'

Meddle was very glad indeed when his aunt said she was going out to tea that afternoon. She was not a nice person to live with when she was cross.

'I'm going to see Sally Simple in the next village,' said Aunt Jemima. 'Now, as it's a nice sunny afternoon, you sit out in the garden in the sun. Have tea there if you like, and just keep an eye on the washing on the line to see it doesn't blow away. And do try and be good and sensible, so that I shall feel pleased with you when I come back.'

'Oh, yes, Aunt,' said Meddle, and he meant it. He waved goodbye to his aunt when she went off in her best coat and hat. Then he heaved a big sigh of relief. Now there was no one to scold him for a few hours! He would be so good. He would just show his aunt how good he could be!

'I'll take aunt's rocking chair out into the garden,' he thought. 'It's so comfortable to sit in, and I can rock myself in it whilst I am reading. I'll borrow aunt's library book, too, so that I shan't need to keep her waiting for it when she wants to take it back.'

He carried the rocking-chair into the middle of the lawn. He fetched two cushions from the sitting-room. He found his aunt's library book and sat down to read it, rocking himself in the sun. It was lovely.

At four o'clock he felt hungry, so he went indoors and found some scones and buttered them. Then he found a nice new ginger cake and took that out for his tea as well. He made himself some tea in the silver teapot, put a nice clean tray-cloth on the tray, and one on the little table beside the rocking-chair, and then sat down to enjoy his tea.

'Aunt Jemima would be pleased to see me having my tea in such a nice way, with a tray-cloth on, and the silver teapot and all,' thought Meddle. 'She is always telling me I'm untidy and careless and messy. She just ought to see how well I am behaving this afternoon, when she isn't here to see me!'

He had his tea and enjoyed it, reading all the time. His book was so exciting that he couldn't be bothered to wash up the tea-things and clear everything away just then. He would do that afterwards.

He suddenly felt cold. The sun had gone behind an enormous black cloud. Meddle looked up and a big drop of rain fell on his nose, making him jump.

'Oooh! It's going to rain!' said Meddle, annoyed. 'I thought it suddenly felt cold. Poor Aunt Jemima – she will just be coming home, and how wet she will get! Her new hat will be soaked. She will probably get an awful cold. Poor Aunt Jemima – no mackintosh, no umbrella!'

Then an idea came into his head and he jumped with delight. 'Of course – I'll go and meet her, and I'll take her mackintosh and umbrella with me. How pleased she will be! What a good idea! I can just get to the station in time to meet the home-coming train.'

Meddle dashed indoors and found his aunt's big blue mackintosh. He took her enormous red umbrella, and went into the front garden and put it up. Splish-splash, pitter-patter, how the rain came down! The drops were huge.

'Dear, dear,' said Meddle, running down the road to the station. 'How wet Aunt Jemima would have got if I hadn't thought of taking her mackintosh and umbrella! How pleased she will be with me! I can be very kind and thoughtful when I like!'

The train puffed in as Meddle got to the station. He rushed on to the platform and looked for his aunt to get out of the train. But she didn't get out. She didn't seem to be there at all.

'She must have missed the train!' thought Meddle. 'Oh dear, there isn't another one for a whole hour. I'd better wait, because the rain is even heavier now.'

So he sat down on the platform and waited. He waited and he waited. The hand of the clock crept all round the figure, and at last the hour was gone. The next train came in and Meddle jumped to his feet. At last!

But dear me, there was no Aunt Jemima on that train, either. It was most puzzling. Meddle didn't know what to do. He really couldn't wait any more. Why, it was seven o'clock. Aunt Jemima must be staying the night with Sally Simple. What a waste of time it had been, waiting about in the cold station!

He went out of the station, feeling cross. The rain was still pouring down, and it wetted his legs. There were enormous puddles everywhere now, and Meddle wished he had remembered to change his house slippers for rubber boots. He had rushed out just as he was. 'Well, I'll put on Aunt's mackintosh, now she won't want it,' he thought. So he put it on, and looked very funny in it, for it came almost down to his big feet, and was much too big for him. He put up the big red umbrella and set off home, grumbling to himself.

He got to the front door, when, to his enormous surprise, it was flung open, and there was his aunt, glaring at him.

'Meddle! Where have you been all this time – and with my mackintosh and umbrella, too. I've been looking for you everywhere. WHERE HAVE YOU BEEN?'

'Oh, Aunt – I'm so surprised to see you,' said Meddle, and he was.

'I said "WHERE HAVE YOU BEEN?"' said his aunt, angrily.

'To the station, to meet you!' said poor Meddle. 'It began to rain so I thought I'd meet you and take your mackintosh and umbrella for you. I thought you'd be glad to see me at the station.'

'What's the sense of meeting the train when you knew I was coming home by bus?' snorted his aunt. And then Meddle suddenly remembered that his aunt always went by bus to Sally Simple's and back, because it passed her door and Sally's too!

'Oh, dear me,' he said, and felt very silly.

'I should think it is "Oh dear me!"' said Aunt Jemima, in a nasty sort of voice. 'That's what I said when I jumped off the bus outside the door, ran in – and found you had left all

32

my nice washing out on the line to get wet. It's soaking now – and the mud has splashed up from the ground and made it all dirty again! Why didn't you take it in when it rained?'

'Well, dear me,' said Meddle, feeling very awkward about it. 'Yes, I should have done that, of course.'

'And why did you have to leave my best rocking-chair, and my two nice sitting-room cushions out in the rain, too?' enquired his

aunt. 'Did you have to leave out my silver tea-things – and the rest of the ginger cake, which is now nothing but wet crumbs?'

'Good gracious me!' said Meddle, feeling even more uncomfortable.

'And I suppose you thought it was a very good idea to leave my library book out in the pouring rain, too?' said Aunt Jemima, her voice getting louder and louder, and her face getting redder and redder.

.Meddle began to feel alarmed. Had he really done all that? And he had meant to be so good and helpful.

'Well,' he said, 'well, Aunt, I did take your mackintosh and umbrella to the station for you.'

'So clever,' said his aunt, 'so clever! When I got home and wanted to go and take in my washing and the tea-things and chair and cushions and book, I looked for my mackintosh and umbrella to keep me dry – but no, they were gone. You had taken them to put on somebody who wasn't there, and you kept nice and dry while I got soaking wet going out into the garden! Meddle, my hand is longing to pinch you!'

'Ooh!' said Meddle, and ran straight out

into the garden, mackintosh, umbrella and all.

'I can wait till you come in!' called his aunt. 'I'll warm you up nicely then. I can wait!'

Poor Meddle. He meant so well, didn't he? He's still out there in the rain, but he'll have to go indoors some time – and then what a scolding he will get!

Chapter 4

Mr Meddle Gets
a Shock

Once it happened that Mr Meddle had
ten pounds sent him for his birthday.
He was so surprised and delighted that he
simply didn't know what to do.

'I think I really must go round to my friend
Jinky and tell him about it,' said Mr Meddle.
'Perhaps he will have some good ideas what
to spend it on.'

So off to Jinky's he went. He showed him
the ten-pound note.

'But I can't think what to spend it on,
Jinky,' said Meddle.

'Well, I can tell you!' said Jinky. 'You want a
new tie and a new coat, a new pair of socks

36

and a new handkerchief. Why don't you buy those?'

'Can I get all that for ten pounds?' asked Meddle, very pleased. 'Oh, that would be fine! Shouldn't I feel grand!'

'I'll come and help you to buy them,' said Jinky, and he got up and the two of them went off to the shop.

Well, you should have seen Meddle when he came out! He had on a new red coat, a yellow tie, a pair of blue socks, and a green-spotted handkerchief! He felt so grand that he could hardly walk!

'Do you feel too grand to walk along with me?' asked Jinky.

'Well, it's a pity you've got such old clothes on – but I'll walk a little way,' said Meddle grandly. 'Is my tie straight, Jinky? Does my handkerchief show enough? Are my socks pulled up straight? Dear me, I wish I could meet the Queen today. I guess she'd wonder who I was.'

Meddle walked along the road, his nose in the air, stepping out in a very important manner. Jinky ran beside him, wishing that he, too, had some new clothes.

'If I met the Queen I would bow like this,'

said Meddle, bowing very suddenly just as an old lady was passing. She looked startled. 'And I would hold out my hand like this, and say, "How do you do, Your Majesty? It is a pleasure to meet you".'

The old lady scuttled away, thinking that Meddle must be quite mad.

Meddle walked along again, talking. 'And then the Queen would say to me, "Ah, how do you do, Meddle? How grand you are looking today! Wherever do you buy such beautiful clothes?"'

'Mind where you are walking, Meddle,' said

Jinky anxiously, seeing that they were coming to where a dirty old coal-van was standing near the pavement.

'Don't interrupt me, Jinky,' said Meddle crossly. 'As I was saying, the Queen would want to know where I got such fine clothes. And I would say, "Your Majesty, come with me and I will buy you a handkerchief just like mine." And the Queen would say, "No, Meddle – you come with me. Just step into my carriage, my dear fellow." And I would step into her carriage like this –'

Meddle had got his nose so high in the air that he didn't see he was passing an open coal-hole, down which the coalman had been emptying coal into a cellar. He stepped right into the hole, and fell down into black darkness!

'This isn't the Queen's carriage!' said Meddle in surprise. 'Where am I? I was just stepping into a carriage – and now I'm here, in a dark, dirty prison!'

Jinky hadn't seen Meddle step into the coal-hole, for he was a little way in front. He turned round to speak to Meddle – and, dear me, Meddle wasn't there! He just simply wasn't there! The only person in the street was a coalman just emptying a sack of coal down a coal-hole!

'Good gracious!' said Jinky, most surprised. 'Where has Meddle gone? He has simply vanished into thin air! What a very extraordinary thing!'

Jinky hurried on to see if by any chance Meddle had got in front of him – and round the corner what should he meet but the Queen's carriage, with the Queen herself inside!

'Look at that now!' said Jinky astonished. 'The Queen and her carriage! Meddle wanted to meet them – and now's his chance. Meddle! Meddle! Where are you? Here's the Queen!'

Meddle was down the coal-hole, of course –
and a sack of coal had just been emptied on
to his surprised head! He was covered in coal-
dust from head to foot! Poor old Meddle!

When the coal came tumbling down,
Meddle was very angry. 'Stop it!' he cried.
'Stop throwing stones at me! Who is it
treating me like this? Wait till I get hold of
you!'

That was the last sack of coal. The coal-man
went back to his van with his sack. And at that
moment Jinky came along crying, 'Meddle!
Meddle! Here's the Queen!'

Meddle looked up and saw the open coal-
hole above him. He began to climb out, eager
to see the Queen. But when Jinky saw a dirty
creature appearing suddenly at his feet, he
was full of terror. He turned and fled,
shouting, 'A monster! A monster!'

Meddle thought Jinky had gone mad. He
climbed out just as the Queen's carriage
came rolling by. Up stepped Meddle and took
off his hat. He held out his soot-covered
hand. 'How do you do, Your Majesty?' he said
in a very grand and polite tone.

But the Queen didn't answer as she ought
to have done. She stared coldly at Meddle

and said, 'Who is this dirty man? Go home and have a bath!'

And the carriage drove on, leaving Meddle staring after it, puzzled and hurt. He set off home, wondering what the matter was. He didn't know he was covered with coal-dust. He thought that he looked as grand as ever, in his new red coat, tie, handkerchief and socks!

He came to Jinky's house and went in to see what had happened to his friend. But when Jinky opened the door and saw the soot-covered creature standing there, he fled away to his kitchen in a fright.

'He's after me, he's after me!' squealed poor Jinky.

'Who's after you?' called Meddle in astonishment, and he went to see. In the hall was a long mirror, and for the first time Meddle saw himself all dirty. He didn't know he was looking at himself, and he stared in horror.

'He's after me, too,' yelled Meddle, and he tore out of the house and went home as fast as ever he could. And then, when he saw his own face looking at him out of his glass at home, quite filthy, he knew what had happened!

'I fell down a coal-hole,' groaned Meddle. 'I was feeling too high and mighty – and I fell down the coal-hole. It serves me right. What must the Queen think of me? Oh dear, oh dear – she'll never, never ask me to ride in her carriage now! Never, never!'

And Meddle was right. The Queen certainly never did!

Chapter 5

Mr Meddle and his Handkerchief

When Meddle went to stay with his Aunt Jemima he always had to be on his best behaviour. One of the things he had to be careful about was coughing.

'Always cough into your hanky, Meddle,' his aunt would say. 'Decent people always do – nasty people don't.'

'Oh,' said Meddle, thinking that his aunt must often have thought him a nasty person. 'Well, I'll try, Aunt Jemima. But I haven't always a hanky with me.'

'Well, you must put a hanky into your pocket every morning,' said his aunt.

'I haven't got a pocket,' said Meddle. 'You

sewed them all up because you said I kept
putting my hands into them.'

'Well, pin a hanky to the front of you,' said
his aunt.

'No, certainly not,' said Meddle. 'People
would laugh when they saw me.'

'Well, put your hanky into the top of your
socks then, or down your neck – anywhere
you can get it if you feel you are going to
cough,' said his aunt.

So Meddle fetched a hanky, and put it
down his neck, just under the top of his blue
vest. Now he could easily get it if he coughed.

He didn't cough all the morning. He
didn't sneeze, either. That afternoon his
Aunt Jemima said: 'Meddle, I am going out
to a meeting this afternoon. It is a meeting
of some very, very good people, who are
going to give money so that we may teach
disadvantaged children. Now, you just show
what nice manners you have – hand round
the cakes at tea – and put chairs for everyone
– and answer nicely when you are spoken to.'

'I don't feel I have nice enough manners
for a meeting like that,' said Meddle. But his
aunt would not let him stay at home. She took
him with her, and he had to go. He was afraid

of his Aunt Jemima because she always said Meddle was still young enough to be scolded.

So he went. He tried to behave nicely. He put chairs for everyone. He looked at the cakes on the tea-table and decided that he would hand a few to himself as well as to other people. He answered very nicely when he was spoken to.

'Now, there's a very nicely behaved nephew of yours,' everyone said to Aunt Jemima. 'You must be proud of him. If only all children were brought up like Meddle, what a wonderful thing it would be!'

Everything went well until tea-time. Then Meddle began to hand round the cakes as he

46

had been told. Then he was asked to take cups of tea to people. He took a cup in one hand and a cup in the other.

He was just walking across the room when he felt a sneeze or cough coming. He didn't know which. It might quite well be both!

'My hanky!' thought Meddle in dismay. 'Did I bring one? Yes, thank goodness I did. I put it down the top of my vest, didn't I? Oh, I shall burst if I don't sneeze or cough soon.'

He had to put down the cups of tea quickly. He pushed one into Mrs Plumpy's lap, and it spilt all over her new purple dress. He shot the other at Miss Skinny, and it scalded her hand. They both squealed loudly.

Everyone looked at Meddle, which was a great pity, because Meddle was doing surprising things. He was trying to find his hanky – and it wasn't where he had put it! He was feeling about in his vest, but there was no hanky there!

'Meddle! Whatever are you doing?' said his Aunt Jemima in horror. 'Have you got a mouse down your front, or what?'

Meddle couldn't answer, because he was trying to keep his cough inside him till he found his hanky. He looked at his aunt, and his face went red and then purple. Everyone felt alarmed.

'He's going mad!' whispered Mrs Plumpy to Miss Skinny.

'Perhaps I put my hanky into my sock,' thought Meddle, in despair. So he pulled up his trouser-ends and felt about in his socks. He took off his shoes, and then his socks, trying to see if the hanky had slipped into the foot. But it wasn't there.

'Meddle! Are you mad?' cried his aunt. 'How can you behave like this?'

Meddle nearly burst himself with trying not to cough or sneeze. 'I did put my hanky in my vest,' he thought. 'I know I did. It must have slipped down. I'll take off my coat and waistcoat and see if I can find it.'

So, to everyone's horror, Meddle took off his coat and flung it on the floor. Then he took off his waistcoat and that went on the floor, too.

'Poor creature, he is quite mad!' said everyone, and they looked with pity at Meddle's aunt, who was now very red in the face, and felt most ashamed of Meddle.

'This is not the time to undress, Meddle,' she said, very sharply.

Meddle was angry. He opened his mouth to say that he was not undressing, he was only trying to find his hanky – and, of course, as soon as he opened his mouth the cough and the sneeze came out together.

'*A-whoosh-ooooooooooooooooooo!*'

Everyone jumped. Meddle suddenly beamed with delight.

'Here's my hanky!' he said, and he waved it in the air. 'It was at the bottom of my vest instead of at the top!'

'Go to the kitchen,' said his aunt, angrily.

'You are not fit to be here with us. You need to be taught more manners than little children. I am really ashamed of you, Meddle.'

Meddle was surprised. He stared at his aunt. 'But you told me only to sneeze or cough into my hanky,' he said, 'and I was only trying to find my hanky. You see, I put it in the top of my vest – and it slipped right down to here – and oh –'

'That will do, Meddle,' said his aunt. 'We don't want to listen to you. We don't want to see you any more today. Carry all these tea-things to the kitchen, and wash up the dishes. That is the least you can do to make up for your very bad behaviour.'

Meddle was angry and hurt, but he didn't like to say anything more, when so many people were glaring at him. He had had no tea himself, and he thought it was very hard that no one offered him any.

Meddle finished the washing up and sat and looked at the cakes that were left. He felt hungry. There were plenty of sandwiches left, too.

'Well, I do think I might have a reward for trying to sneeze and cough into my hanky, and for washing up the tea-things,' he said at last.

So he ate up all the sandwiches, two ginger cakes, three shortbreads, four pieces of sponge cake, and six chocolate biscuits.

He went home with his aunt later on. 'Well,' said Meddle, 'thanks for taking me, Aunt. I did enjoy the meeting.'

But his aunt never knew why, and he didn't tell her! Poor old Meddle, he does his best, but somehow he always makes a muddle, doesn't he!

Chapter 6

Mr Meddle Loses his Temper

Now once when Mr Meddle came home from doing his shopping, he found a van outside his gate, and a man putting a whole lot of boxes and trunks in his front garden.

'Hey!' shouted Mr Meddle. 'What are you putting those things in my garden for? Take them away.'

'I'm putting them in the garden because I can't make anyone hear in the house,' said the man, putting another box into the garden. 'These things are labelled for your house. I can't get them into the house so I'm leaving them in the garden.'

'Oh, no, you're not!' cried Meddle. 'It's a mistake. These are not for me. I've ordered nothing from any shop. Take them out again!'

'I've spent all my time putting them in and I'm *not* going to take them out again!' said the man, slamming down a large parrot-cage with an angry parrot inside.

'I say! I don't want that awful parrot!' yelled Mr Meddle, losing his temper. 'Stop, stop! Don't put any more things in here.'

'That's the last!' said the man, and he put down a large round hat-box. 'Good day to you!'

He climbed up into his van and drove off down the street. Meddle was so angry that he went purple in the face. He picked up the hat-box and threw it after the man.

It rolled down the street after him. It broke open and three big hats with red, pink, and yellow flowers on them shot out of the box into the gutter.

'Good!' said Meddle fiercely. 'Stay there, hats!'

He looked at all the things messing up his garden.

The parrot glared at him and he glared back at the parrot.

53

The big bird unexpectedly began to sing, swaying to and fro on its perch,

> *'Yankee doodle came to town,*
> *Upon a little pony!'*

sang the parrot. Then he broke off to look rudely at Meddle, and said. 'Go and brush your hair! Go and brush your hair!'

'Now look here,' said Meddle in a fine temper, 'I won't have parrots telling me what to do! Be quiet! Brush your own hair!'

'Yankee doodle, go and wash your face!'

said the parrot, and then it put back its head and laughed with a loud screech. Meddle went to the cage, took hold of it, and carried it to the gate. He threw it over the gate into the road. Crash! The cage hit the ground, the parrot let out a squawk, and then began to call Meddle all kinds of rude names.

'Well, what a morning, what a morning!' shouted Meddle in a fury. 'Things all over my garden! Parrots telling me to wash my face! Hats in the gutter! I won't have it!'

He caught up a small box and sent that flying over the hedge. Smash! It hit the ground, burst open, and spilt white stockings all over the road.

'White socks!' said Meddle in amazement. 'Who in the world wears white stockings now! Well, here goes!'

He sent another box flying over the hedge. It spilt open and soap, scent, toothbrushes, creams, hair-pins, and all kinds of things burst out of it. Meddle giggled. It was funny to see such an odd crowd of things in the road. Then he went quite mad and threw everything else over the hedge too.

Bang! That was a big trunk. Crash! That was a wooden box. Smash! That was a bag with something breakable inside. My word, what a game!

'That'll teach people to pile up my garden with things that don't belong to me!' cried Meddle, thoroughly enjoying himself.

By this time quite a crowd had come along and every one was watching Meddle in greatest surprise.

'Help yourselves!' cried Meddle, looking over the gate. 'They don't belong to me! Help yourselves!'

At this moment a cab drew up near by and a rather fat old woman looked out. She saw Meddle and waved to him.

'Meddle, Meddle! I'm so pleased to see you! I hope you didn't forget I was coming today to stay with you. You wrote me such a nice letter – but you're so forgetful, aren't you!'

Meddle stared at the large old lady getting out of the cab, with a big umbrella and red bag.

'AUNT JEMIMA!' he cried. 'Ohhhh-hhhhhhhh!'

Aunt Jemima looked round and saw the crowd of people. She saw the trunks, bags, and boxes in the road, spilt and bursting. She saw the parrot's cage, all on one side with the parrot squawking for all he was worth:

'Go and clean your teeth! Go and clean your teeth!'

'My parrot!' screamed Aunt Jemima. 'Who put him out there in the road, all on one side!'

'Meddle threw him over the gate,' said someone.

'THREW HIM OVER THE GATE!' said Aunt Jemima in a truly dreadful voice. 'And

who threw all these boxes and trunks of mine
out here?'

'Meddle did!' shouted everyone.

'MEDDLE! Do you mean to say that you
threw all my goods into the road like this?'
said his Aunt Jemima, her red face going
even redder.

'I forgot you were c-c-c-coming, Aunt
Jemima,' stammered Meddle. 'A man
brought these things into my garden when I
was out, and I d-d-d-d-didn't think of them
being yours. I lost my t-t-t-temper and threw
them over the hedge.'

'Meddle, I'm going to lose my temper too,'
said Aunt Jemima. 'When you were a naughty,
meddlesome little boy, I had to scold you –
and, Meddle, I feel that's what I'm going to
do now. Come here!'

But Meddle didn't come. He went! Down
the street he went like lightening. His Aunt
Jemima snorted.

'Well, I can wait till he comes back,' she
said. 'Cabman, pick up all these things and
take them into this house for me. I'll take the
parrot, poor darling.'

'Go and clean your shoes! Go and clean
your shoes!' said the parrot softly, and tried

to rub its head against Aunt Jemima's fingers.

'You clever thing,' said Aunt Jemima. 'Wait till I get hold of Meddle. I'll teach him to throw parrots into the road. Lost his temper indeed! Wait till he sees me lose mine! He'll get a fine shock!'

Poor Meddle! He doesn't dare to go home – and Aunt Jemima is quite determined to stay till he does. So what's going to happen, do you think?

Chapter 7

Mr Meddle Makes a Mistake

Once Mr Meddle went out to a party at Mistress Penny's. The streets were very dark, for there were no street lights on. Meddle took his torch with him – but, oh dear, what a nuisance! He had forgotten it was broken.

'Now I meant to get that mended this morning!' said Meddle. 'How foolish I am! I do hope I shall get safely to Mistress Penny's.'

Just then Mr Geeky went by, flashing his torch on the ground. Meddle was pleased.

'Hi, Mr Geeky!' he called. 'Are you going to Mistress Penny's party? Can I come with you? My torch is broken.'

'Come along then,' said Mr Geeky, and he flashed his torch at Mr Meddle. Meddle ran up to him and together they went along the road to Mistress Penny's. It was fun to be going to a party.

It was a lovely party. There were plenty of good things to eat. There were three chocolate cakes, six pink jellies, some egg sandwiches, and a fruit salad with a big jug of cream. Really, Meddle didn't know when he had enjoyed himself more!

There were games to play, and after a while Mistress Penny cleared away the chairs, rolled up the carpet, and said they could dance. She set the record player going, and everybody began to dance.

At ten o'clock some of the guests began to go home. Meddle didn't. He always liked to stay till the very, very last.

But at twelve o'clock even he had to go, because there was nothing more left to eat and drink, and Mistress Penny wanted to go to bed. So Meddle put on his hat and coat and looked round for Mr Geeky.

But Mr Geeky had gone home long before. 'Oh dear!' said Meddle in dismay. 'He had the torch! Mine is broken. I really can't go home in the dark.'

'You'll have to, Meddle,' said Mistress

Penny at once. She didn't want to have Meddle staying the night at her house. She knew what an old meddler he was!

'Oh well, I suppose I shall find my way all right,' said Meddle. He said goodbye to Mistress Penny, and went carefully down the path to the gate. He came to the gate before he expected, and walked straight into it. Oh, what a bruise he would have on his knees tomorrow!

Meddle groaned and rubbed his knees. Then he stepped on to the pavement and

made his way slowly up the road. He walked into a black cat, who spat at him and scratched his leg. He fell off the kerb at least three times, and sat down heavily in the gutter! Poor Meddle!

At last he came to his own street. At least, he thought it was! It wasn't really, but it was so dark that Meddle didn't know it was the wrong street. His house was the third one in his street, so Meddle counted the front gates he came to.

'One, gate – two gates – three gates. This is my house! Good!'

He went in at the gate, and walked up the path to the front door. He took out his door-key.

It didn't fit at all! He could not make it turn in the lock – so the door remained shut and couldn't be opened. Meddle was very angry.

'What's the matter with the key?' he said. 'Why doesn't it open the door? What a nuisance for it to go wrong at this time of night! Now what am I do do?'

He stood and thought hard. 'I'd better go and see if the back window is open,' he said. 'I could get in that way.'

So he stumbled round to the back, falling over a dustbin in the way. He came to the back window and tried to see if it would open. Yes! It would! Good! Now he could get in and go to bed.

So he climbed in through the window, and got into the kitchen. He felt about for a lamp, but he couldn't find one.

'Well, I really did think there was one on the kitchen table,' thought Meddle, vexed. 'I suppose there wasn't after all. Well, I must go up to bed without a light.'

He found the stairs and tumbled up them. He came to the top, and tried to find the handle of his door. It didn't seem to be in the right place somehow. But at last he did find a door-handle, turned it, and went into the bedroom. The first thing he did was to walk straight into the bed!

'Now, the bed shouldn't be just here, surely!' said Meddle in astonishment. 'It should be over in the corner. Who's been meddling with my room whilst I've been out? Just wait till I catch them! Putting my bed out in the middle of the room like this!'

He undressed himself in the dark, still grumbling. He felt round for the bedside table, but that seemed to be in the wrong place too! Most extraordinary!

At last he got into bed. He fell asleep almost at once, for he was very tired. He slept until the sun was quite high in the sky, and then he woke up and opened his eyes.

He was most astonished at what he saw. The walls were a bright pink. Meddle knew quite well that his usual wall-paper was pale green with a pattern of leaves.

He looked round the room. There was a pink carpet on the floor. Meddle knew he had only one green rug. There was an arm-chair with two cushions. Meddle's room had no armchair at all. The bed was wide and comfortable, and had on it a beautiful pink silk cover, two pink blankets, and pink sheets.

Meddle looked at everything and marvelled to see it. 'This is magic,' he said. 'Real live magic! I go to bed in my own little green bedroom, and I wake up in a most beautiful pink one, with armchair and cushions, and the most comfortable bed I've every slept in! Magic! Yes, wonderful magic!'

He lay in the soft bed and enjoyed himself. He felt hungry and wondered about breakfast. Perhaps there were servants in his changed house, who could cook for him a marvellous breakfast. Oooh! How fine that would be!

There was a bell near by in the wall. Meddle pressed it hard. It went 'Ting-g-g-g-g!' very loudly indeed. Nobody came, though Meddle could quite well hear somebody moving about downstairs. He pressed the bell hard again – 'Ting-g-g-g-g-g-g-g!'

Then he heard a voice exclaiming downstairs, 'There's that bell again! There's nobody at the front door and nobody at the back. Whoever can be ringing the bell?'

Ting-g-g-g-g-g!' Meddle rang it again, feeling quite cross. There was the sound of footsteps coming upstairs. 'I do believe it's my spare-room bell!' said a voice, and in came a woman, with a red overall tied round her.

Meddle stared at her. 'Bring me some breakfast, please,' he said.

'WELL!' said the woman in a most angry and astonished voice. 'WELL! And what may you be doing here, I should like to know, in my best spare-room bed?'

'I don't know what you are talking about,' said Meddle crossly. 'Bring me some breakfast. I'm hungry.'

'Well, hungry you'll have to be!' said the woman, and she tipped Meddle out of his warm bed. 'How dare you sleep here! You wicked fellow! Get out of my house at once!'

'Madam!' said Meddle angrily, 'How dare you treat me like this in my own house!' He climbed back into bed again. The woman at once tipped him out. She took hold of poor Meddle, who was dressed only in his best shirt, and walked him firmly to the top of the stairs. She gave him a push.

Down rolled Meddle, bumping from step to step. The woman ran down after him. She opened the front door and pushed him out into the garden.

'I'm going to get a policeman!' cried poor Mr Meddle. 'I will not be turned out of my house like this.' And off he rushed to find a policeman.

He ran up and down the streets for a long time before he could find Mr Plod the policeman. Mr Plod was surprised to see Mr Meddle in his best shirt and nothing else. And he was even more surprised to hear Meddle's story.

'You come along to my house and see this nasty woman,' begged Meddle. So Mr Plod went along to Mr Meddle's house; and as it was daylight, they went to the right house this time – Mr Meddle's own proper house.

And, of course, there was nobody there at all – no woman, no pink bedroom, no room with pink wall-paper! Mr Meddle couldn't believe his eyes.

'But where are my clothes?' he said. 'I know I left them in the pink bedroom, Mr Plod, because I saw them there this morning. Oh, Mr Plod, where are my clothes?'

But Mr Plod didn't know. He thought Mr Meddle was very silly. He left him and went down the road and up the next one. And there, on the pavement, he was very much surprised to see the rest of Meddle's clothes! The woman had thrown them out of the window after Mr Meddle, and there they were.

'More and more peculiar,' said Mr Plod, and he took them back to Meddle. 'Now don't you come along to me with any more silly stories,' he said sternly, and he looked so cross that Meddle shivered and shook.

And to this day Meddle doesn't know what really happened. Isn't he an old silly, really?

Chapter 8

Mr Meddle and his Aunt's Cat

Once Meddle went to stay with his Aunt Tabitha. He quite liked her, because she could make the most delicious chocolate puddings, and when she was in a good temper she used to make ice-creams that were almost too good to be true.

But what Meddle didn't like was his aunt's cat, Cinders. Cinders was a big black cat, with twenty sharp claws, and whiskers that stuck out straight from each side of his mouth.

'Cinders glares at me as if he simply hates me,' Meddle complained.

'I'm not surprised,' said Aunt Tabitha.

'You've trodden on his tail at least six times this morning.'

'Well, he shouldn't leave it lying about,' said Meddle. 'He should curl it round him like sensible cats do. He will leave it lying straight out. And I do think, Aunt Tabitha, that you should teach Cinders better manners. Do you know, he spat at me yesterday. Well, you've always told me that spitting is very, very rude.'

'So it is,' said his aunt, 'but I'm not at all surprised at Cinders being rude to you. You stepped right into his bowl of milk and upset it. And what's more, you didn't bother to get a cloth and wipe it up.'

'Well, that would have been a waste,' said Meddle. 'I didn't see why Cinders shouldn't lick up the milk off the floor himself, instead of my wiping it up. You're always telling me not to waste things.'

'That's enough,' said his aunt. 'And don't come complaining to me any more about Cinders' behaviour. He doesn't complain about yours!'

'Well, if Cinders dares to complain about me, I'll – I'll – I'll –' began Meddle.

'You'll put him in the dustbin, I suppose,'

71

said Aunt Tabitha, crossly. 'Well, you won't. If I hear of you daring to punish my dear, darling Cinders, I'll send you to bed for two days!'

So Meddle didn't dare touch Cinders, however much he longed to. He just glared at him whenever he passed him, and Cinders glared back.

Now, Meddle's Aunt Tabitha was very good about collecting paper for recycling. She kept a big sack into which every single bit of wastepaper was put, and when it was full, the dustman collected it. Meddle watched it getting fuller and fuller, and he was most interested in it. He put every bit of paper into it that he could.

'But, Meddle, don't put in today's paper before I've even read it!' said his aunt. 'And, dear me, where is my writing pad? Surely to goodness you haven't put that in? Dear, dear, what a silly fellow you are. I don't know how I put up with you.'

One day the sack really was full. Meddle felt sure it could be tied up and sent away. So he went to get some string from his aunt. Whilst he was gone, the cat jumped up on to the sack, and sniffed it. He always liked paper. It was soft and warm, and made a lovely noise. Cinders slipped himself right down into the sack, and scrabbled about happily. Then he made himself a nice cosy place and went to sleep.

When Meddle came back with the string he had no idea at all that Cinders had put himself into the sack. He tied up the neck firmly and then dragged the sack outside for the dustman to collect. Cinders woke up and felt most astonished at being dragged along like that. He stuck his claws out through the sacking and scratched Meddle's hand.

'Ow!' said Meddle, in pain. 'There's

something sharp in that sack. Aunt Tabitha must have put in her needle-case by mistake, or something. Horrid old sack!'

Meddle gave it a punch, and the cat yowled. That gave Meddle such a fright that he dropped the sack in a hurry by the dustbin, and fled indoors.

'Funny sort of sack,' he thought, as he bathed his bleeding hand. 'It scratches me, and then yowls. I'm glad it's going.'

Now Cinders was most annoyed at not being able to get out of the sack. He jumped and scrabbled, he wriggled and struggled. He

yowled and mewed, and made the sack sway about in the most alarming manner. When the lady next door came out into her yard, she was most astonished to see the sack behaving like this. She watched it in surprise.

The dustman came to collect it after a while, and the lady called to him: 'You be careful of that sack! It's alive!'

'Ha, ha! Funny joke!' said the dustman, and hoisted the sack on to his shoulder. That was too much for Cinders. He let out a yowl like a siren going off, and dug all twenty claws through the sack into the dustman's shoulder. The man gave a yelp of surprise, and dropped the sack. Cinders leapt about inside it, and the sack jumped here and there in a most surprising manner.

'Well, I never saw a sack behaving like that before,' said the dustman, scratching his head. 'Yowling and scratching and jumping. I'll complain to the lady. I can't collect a sack that behaves like that.'

So he knocked at the kitchen door and complained bitterly to Aunt Tabitha. She was most surprised.

'But it's only a sackful of paper,' she said. 'I know, because I saw every bit of paper that was put into it. Come, come, my man, don't be silly.'

'Mee-ow, mee-ow!' said the sack, and did a few jumps round the yard.

'There you are,' said the dustman. 'You had better undo your sack, lady, and see what's the matter with it. It's my belief there's a tiger or a lion inside!'

'What nonsense!' said Aunt Tabitha. She fetched a knife and cut the string at the neck. Out jumped Cinders with another yowl, and a mass of bits of paper flew out after him. The dustman ran out of the back gate and didn't come back. The neighbour flew into her kitchen and slammed the door.

'Why, it's Cinders!' cried Aunt Tabitha, in surprise. 'My dear, Darling Cinders! Meddle, Meddle, why did you tie up Cinders in the paper sack? You bad, wicked fellow, you wanted to get rid of Cinders, so you thought of sending him away in the sack! Oh, wait till I get you! I'll put you into a sack; so I will!'

Poor Meddle! He was well scolded by his aunt, and then he had to go to bed for two days. His Aunt Tabitha simply would not believe that he didn't know Cinders was in the sack.

Meddle wouldn't have minded staying in bed at all, for he was a lazy fellow – but Cinders would sit on his window-sill and wash himself all the time. In between his washing he glared at Meddle out of his bright green eyes.

'And I daren't even throw my toothbrush at him!' groaned Meddle. 'Go away, Cinders, you nasty, glaring cat. Go away! I really will put you into a sack if you don't.'

'No-eeow, you-eeow, won't-ee-ow,' said Cinders, quite clearly. It really was rather hard luck for poor old Meddle, wasn't it?

Chapter 9

Now, Mr Meddle!

Just over the farmer's fence was a fine big plum tree, full of ripe purple plums. The boys of the village knew this tree well, and each summer they came along to try to get the plums.

They had to keep a good look-out for the farmer and his dog. Once two boys had been caught and the farmer had scolded them well, which served them right. Now they didn't dare to get over the fence into the field. They just tried to knock down the plums that hung above the fence.

'Come on – throw stones up, or bits of wood,' said Harry, picking up a big stone. He threw it into the plum tree, and knocked down a plum. It also broke a small branch, which fell into the road.

'Pity that branch hasn't got plums on!' said Jack. 'I say – that's an idea – let's throw up something to break the branches – then maybe we'll get a lot of plums at once if the branches fall down our side.'

Leonard went to get some walking-sticks from his home nearby. Soon the boys were flinging up the sticks and breaking the smaller, very brittle branches easily. Down they came, some with plums on them.

Now Mr Meddle happened to come along the road just about then. Of course, when he saw the little crowd of boys with sticks, he went up at once. He loved to meddle in anything.

'Ha! That's a silly thing to do, to try to pick plums by throwing sticks!' said Meddle. 'Why don't you be sensible, and climb the tree?'

'We're afraid to,' said Jack, thinking of the farmer and his dog.

'What! A great boy like you afraid of climbing a tree!' said Meddle. 'Good gracious! When I was a boy I always climbed trees. I wasn't afraid! I could climb that tree in two shakes of a duck's tail!'

Harry winked at the others. 'You couldn't!' he said. 'I bet you, you couldn't!'

'I'll just show you then!' said Meddle. 'And what's more, I'll pick the plums for you so that you don't damage the tree any more. Now see how well I can shin up this plum tree!'

He climbed over the fence, and shinned up the plum tree. The boys pretended to admire him, and shouted loudly, 'Jolly good, Mr Meddle! Fine! You went up in a trice! Are there any plums near you?'

'I'll show you how to pick plums!' said Meddle, and he began to throw some down to the boys. They picked them up in glee and filled their pockets. Silly old Meddle – what a thing to do!

Suddenly Meddle noticed that the boys were no longer there. He looked down in surprise. Where had they gone, all of a sudden?

The boys had certainly gone – gone at top speed too – but somebody else was there, under the tree, somebody with an extremely fierce-looking dog!

'Oh – er – good morning, Farmer Straw,' said Meddle, peering between the boughs. 'Er – can I throw you down some plums?'

'Mr Meddle, I'm surprised at you!' said Farmer Straw, in his loud voice. 'Yes, downright surprised at you! Climbing my plum tree and throwing my plums down! What do you mean by it?'

'Nothing,' said Meddle. 'I was merely showing some boys how to pick plums without damaging the tree. You ought to thank me for saving your tree from having its branches broken off by sticks and stones! You ought to give me a reward.'

'Ho! Well, you come on down here and I'll give you a fine reward,' said Farmer Straw, in a roaring kind of voice. 'Come along! You'll have a reward all right. Always meddling in something, aren't you? I suppose it didn't occur to you that the quickest way of saving my tree and its plums would be to drive those boys off? Come on down and have your reward.'

Meddle didn't want to. He didn't like the look of the dog or of the farmer either. He didn't think he would even like the reward, whatever it was. In fact, he thought he would prefer to sit up in the tree the whole of the day rather than go near that most unpleasant-looking dog!

'Well, well! I haven't hours to waste on you, Meddle,' said the farmer. 'I'll leave you here.'

Meddle heaved a sigh of relief when he saw the farmer striding off. He began to climb down the tree. A horrible growl stopped him, and he climbed up again at top speed.

The farmer had gone – but the dog hadn't! 'Grrr-rrr-rrr!' said the dog. 'Meddle by name and Meddle by nature! Just come down and meddle with me. Grrr-rr-rr!'

But Meddle wasn't going to meddle with a snarling dog – so goodness knows how long he'll stay up in that plum tree!

Chapter 10

Mr Meddle Tries to Help

Meddle got up feeling very happy one morning. He sang so loudly in his bath that his Aunt Jemima rapped on the door.

'Meddle! Do stop that dreadful noise. You've frightened the cat out of the house.'

'What dreadful noise?' said Meddle, surprised. 'I was only singing because I feel good and happy this lovely morning.'

'Oh, dear,' said his aunt. 'That means you'll want to help everyone and interfere with everything. I know you, Meddle! Anyway, stop that singing, or whatever it is.'

Meddle came down to breakfast, beaming. 'Now, you tell me anything you want done today,' he said to his aunt. 'I'll do it with pleasure.'

'I don't want your help, thank you,' said Aunt Jemima. 'Last time you helped me you said you'd weed the garden – and you went and pulled up all the little seedlings instead of the weeds. I don't want any more of your help.'

'Well, Aunt – it's not good of you to stop somebody when they want to do a kindness,' said Meddle, offended.

'All right, do your kindness – but go and offer it to someone else, not me,' said his aunt. 'What about old Dame Grumble? She's

hurt one of her feet and can't do her shopping properly. Go and offer to do it for her.'

'I don't like Dame Grumble very much,' said Meddle. 'She's got a sharp tongue.'

'So have I,' said his aunt, 'and I shall use it in a minute if you don't stop putting marmalade on your porridge, Meddle.'

'Oh, dear – I thought I was putting on golden syrup,' said Meddle. 'Well – I'll go and see if Dame Grumble wants any errands running – but I hope she doesn't.'

Off he went round to Dame Grumble's little cottage after breakfast. He found her hobbling about her kitchen, grumbling hard to her old black cat.

'I've a good mind to send you away, Smudge! There you sit, as lazy as anything, and let the mice run all round you at night – and you put yourself in my way so that I fall over you and hurt my foot! And now I've got to go out shopping, and hobble along in pain. For shame, Smudge.'

Smudge took no notice at all, but washed herself all over very carefully. Meddle rapped on the door and Dame Grumble called loudly: 'Come in, come in, don't stand there knocking and knocking. Can't you bring the washing in and put it down on the table for me as usual?'

'No,' said Meddle, stepping inside. 'I'm not the washerwoman. I'm Meddle.'

'And what have you come bothering me for?' asked Dame Grumble. 'Bless the fellow, he's gone and trodden on the cat, already!'

'Well, it shouldn't sit down on a black rug,' said Meddle. 'A black cat should have the sense to sit on a white one. Look how she's scratched me! And all I came for was to ask you if I could do your shopping for you. This is a fine reward for kindness, I must say – a long scratch all down my leg.'

'Pooh – that's nothing,' said Dame Grumble. 'Fancy making a fuss about that. Yes, you can do my errands for me. That's certainly kind of you.'

'What would you like me to do?' asked Meddle, getting as far away from the cat as he could.

'I'd like you to fetch my dog for me,' said Dame Grumble. 'He's at the vet's – the animal doctor, you know. And I want my dress back from the cleaner's.'

'Well – I don't know about getting your

dog,' said Meddle, nervously. 'Is he fierce at all?'

'No, he's a lamb,' said Dame Grumble. 'He's a pet. He never even growls, he's so good-tempered. You can take his lead with you, and he'll follow close to your heel without any trouble at all.'

Well, this sounded all right to Meddle. He felt he could manage a dog like that. 'What about your dress?' he asked.

'That should be quite ready,' said Dame Grumble. 'Here's the ticket for it – it's white with a black collar. And I'll just scribble a note for the vet about the dog. His name is Patch, and he's brown with spots on his back. There you are – you can't possibly make a mistake.'

Meddle put one ticket in his left-hand pocket and one in his right. 'Now I shan't mix them up,' he said. 'Well, goodbye, Dame Grumble. I'll soon be back with your dog and your dress.'

He went off down the road to the vet's. He couldn't make himself heard at the front door, so he went round to the yard where there were cages of dogs of all kinds. They set up a great barking when they saw Meddle.

A worried-looking kennel worker looked round a corner to see what the matter was. 'What do you want?' she said. 'Have you come to fetch a dog?'

'Yes,' said Meddle. 'I want Dame Grumble's dog.'

'What is he like?' asked the girl. 'Could you take him out of his cage yourself, please? I've got a hurt dog here and I can't leave him for a bit.'

'That's all right,' said Meddle, and he fished a bit of paper out of his pocket. 'I've got a description of the dog here. He's white with a black collar. I'll have a look round and see if I can spot him.'

He looked in all the cages. He couldn't see a dog with a white coat and black collar. But at last he came to a very big cage and inside was a grey-white dog wearing a black collar. It was rather a big dog, and Meddle didn't really like the look of it.

'Still, Dame Grumble said it was as quiet as a lamb, and a real pet,' he thought to himself. 'Come along, Patch. Good dog, then, nice dog.'

The dog seemed surprised at Meddle, and even more surprised when his door was

opened and he was let out. Meddle snapped
the lead on to the big dog's collar.

'Come along,' he said. 'Home, doggy,
home!'

The dog growled. Meddle was startled.
'Oh, naughty!' he said. 'Your mistress said
you never growled. Come along now!'

He dragged the dog out of the yard, calling
goodbye to the kennel worker as he went.
Out of the gate he walked, the dog dragging
behind him.

'You're not as well-behaved as your mistress
said you were,' said Meddle, and pulled hard
at the lead. 'Do you want your head pulled

off, silly? I tell you, if it's to be a tug-of-war between us, you won't like it!'

The dog growled so fiercely that Meddle felt alarmed. It sat down hard and Meddle began to despair of ever getting it home. Then he had a bright idea. He saw the butcher's nearby, and felt pleased. 'I'll just tie you to the railings here for a minute,' he told the dog, 'then I'll slip over to the butcher's and buy a big bone. You'll come after me quickly enough then!'

He went to buy a bone. As soon as he came back the dog wagged his tail at him and tried to jump at the bone. Meddle stuffed it into his pocket. 'Now, you just follow me quietly, smelling your bone all the way,' he said. 'And maybe I'll give it to you when we get home.'

The dog trotted after him, jumping at Meddle's pocket and tearing it. Meddle was annoyed. He scolded the dog, which at once showed its teeth in a very alarming manner.

'Here's the cleaners,' said Meddle, relieved. He tied the dog to the fence nearby and disappeared into the shop. He pulled out the other bit of paper from his second pocket.

'I've come for a dress sent to be cleaned for

Dame Grumble,' he said. 'It's – let me see – it's brown with spots on the back.'

'I haven't a brown dress with spots on the back,' said the girl. 'I've a brown dress without spots, though. That must be the one. I expect it was sent to have the spots cleaned off the back.'

'Oh, yes – I expect it was,' said Meddle. 'Can I take it please? I'm in a hurry. I've got a dog waiting outside.'

'You certainly have,' said the girl. 'He's howling the place down. My word – doesn't he look fierce, too?'

'He does rather,' said Meddle, his heart sinking at the sight of the very angry dog. It was almost pulling the fence down in its antics.

'Come on, Patch. We haven't far to go now,' said Meddle, and took the lead again. The dog at once smelt the bone in his pocket and jumped at him. Meddle sat down heavily in a puddle, and dropped the brown dress in the mud. He pushed off the dog and got up, very angry indeed.

'Look what you've done – messed up a nice clean frock belonging to your mistress!' he scolded the dog.

The dog looked as if it was about to knock him over again, so Meddle hastily took the bone out of his pocket and gave it to him. The dog snatched at it and wanted to sit down and eat it straight away. 'No. You come along home,' said Meddle, pulling hard. 'I'm tired of you. Come along.'

Soon a few more dogs joined them, smelling the bone that the big dog carried. Meddle was really frightened. Oh, dear – it looked as if there would be a fine old dog-fight soon. Dame Grumble's dog was growling without stopping now.

Then a woman called out from over the

road in a very angry voice: 'Hey, you! What are you doing with my dog?'

'Which dog's yours?' shouted back Meddle. 'Call him! I don't want all these tiresome animals round me. Call him off.'

'I'll tell a policeman, you robber!' cried the woman. 'Stealing dogs like that!'

Meddle went off, scowling, dragging the big dog behind him with even more difficulty. Six other dogs followed in delight sniffing the delicious bone that the big dog carried.

Poor Meddle was very, very thankful when he reached Dame Grumble's house. He dragged the dog into the kitchen and shut the door.

The dog saw the cat and immediately flew at it. Smudge tore up the grandfather clock and sat there on the top, spitting with rage. The dog jumped at the clock and brought it down with a tremendous crash. The cat leapt to the top of the curtains. Meddle almost jumped out of his skin, and the dog fled under the table in fright.

Dame Grumble came rushing in from the garden. 'What's all this? What's the matter with Smudge? What was that crash? Oh, my beautiful clock! Who knocked it over?'

'Your horrible, snarling, bad-tempered dog,' said Meddle, in a very bad temper himself now. 'Take your nasty animal – and your dress! I've had enough of doing your errands for you!'

He flung the muddy dress on the table and turned to go. 'Oh,' cried Dame Grumble, 'what a dirty dress – and it isn't even mine! Mine was white with a black collar. I told you so!'

At that moment the dog appeared from under the table. Dame Grumble gave a scream. 'What's this dog doing here? He's not mine! What a horrible creature! Mine was brown with spots down his back. I told you so. I even wrote everything down so that you couldn't make a mistake.

Meddle stared at Dame Grumble and felt himself going wobbly at the legs. He looked at the dog and then he looked at the dress. He'd mixed them up – the dog should have been brown with black spots, not the dress; and the dress should have been white with a black collar, not the dog. Oh, dear, oh, dear – now what was he to do?

He crept to the door. He opened it, but before he could escape out of the front gate he marched straight into a big policeman, who was followed by the angry woman who had shouted at him in the street.

The policeman caught hold of his arm. 'I want to know where the dog is that you stole from the kennels,' he said sternly. 'It's been reported to me. Where's that dog?'

'I didn't steal it. It was all a mistake,' said Meddle. The dog appeared at the door and saw its mistress. It rushed to her with whines of delight. Then Dame Grumble appeared and began to talk so loudly to the policeman that Meddle was able to escape. He rushed thankfully back to his Aunt Jemima's and put himself to bed, out of everybody's way.

But that wasn't a bit of good. Dame Grumble, the policeman, the woman and the dog, all came to his aunt's house, and before poor Meddle could even hide in the wardrobe there they were all round his bed!

Now he's got to pay for the grandfather clock being mended, and pay a fine for getting the wrong dog, and pay for the wrong brown dress to be cleaned all over again for its rightful owner. He won't have any pocket-money for a very long time. Poor Meddle.

'That will teach you not to meddle and muddle as you do,' said Aunt Jemima. But it won't. He just can't help it, can he?